A Very Young Skier

Written and Photographed by
Jill Krementz

 Dial Books for Young Readers
New York

Also by Jill Krementz

THE FACE OF SOUTH VIETNAM
(with text by Dean Brelis)

SWEET PEA—A BLACK GIRL GROWING UP
IN THE RURAL SOUTH

WORDS AND THEIR MASTERS
(with text by Israel Shenker)

A VERY YOUNG DANCER

A VERY YOUNG RIDER

A VERY YOUNG GYMNAST

A VERY YOUNG CIRCUS FLYER

A VERY YOUNG SKATER

THE WRITER'S IMAGE

HOW IT FEELS WHEN A PARENT DIES

HOW IT FEELS TO BE ADOPTED

HOW IT FEELS WHEN PARENTS DIVORCE

HOW IT FEELS TO FIGHT FOR YOUR LIFE

THE FUN OF COOKING

LILY GOES TO THE PLAYGROUND

JACK GOES TO THE BEACH

TARYN GOES TO THE DENTIST

BENJY GOES TO A RESTAURANT

KATHERINE GOES TO NURSERY SCHOOL

JAMIE GOES ON AN AIRPLANE

ZACHARY GOES TO THE ZOO

HOLLY'S FARM ANIMALS

A VISIT TO WASHINGTON, D.C.

Published by Dial Books for Young Readers
A Division of Penguin Books USA Inc.
375 Hudson Street
New York, New York 10014

Library of Congress Cataloging in Publication Data
Krementz, Jill.
A very young skier/written and photographed by Jill Krementz.
p. cm.
Summary: Text and photographs introduce a nine-year-old ski
enthusiast from Sun Valley, Idaho.
ISBN 0-8037-0821-1.—ISBN 0-8037-0823-8 (lib. bdg.)
1. Cimino, Stephanie—Juvenile literature.
2. Skiers—United States—Biography—Juvenile literature.
[1. Skis and skiing. 2. Skiers.] I. Title.
GV854.2.C56K74 1990 796.93'092—dc20 [B] 89-28760 CIP AC

With special thanks to

The Cimino family

Ed Downe who introduced me to Jim Cimino,
Stephanie's grandfather

Shannon Besoyan,
Director of Public Relations, Sun Valley Company,
and the entire staff of the Sun Valley Ski School

My assistants, Jerry Hadam and Mike Guryan

All the young skiers and their wonderful families
who made me feel so welcome at Sun Valley.

I don't know if I want to be a competitive skier when I grow up but right now it's my favorite sport. My name is Stephanie Cimino and I live in Sun Valley, Idaho. There are lots of big mountains here so some kids learn to ski as soon as they can walk. I didn't put on skis until I was seven. I'm nine now.

There are two kinds of skiing—Alpine, which is downhill, and Nordic, which is cross-country. I like to do both.

My whole family skis. My Mom, Dad, and my little brother James.

James is four and since he's just learning, he doesn't use poles. With the youngest skiers, it's better if they concentrate on managing their skis without having to think about pole technique at the same time. Since they are so small and close to the ground, the poles aren't very important.

I'm in the third grade and I go to the Ernest Hemingway School. Ernest Hemingway was a famous writer who lived near here until he died. My teacher's name is Mrs. Fitzpatrick. My favorite subjects are math and phys ed.

We get out of school every day at 2:30. Since the mountain doesn't close until 4:00 I have time for lots of runs—or a lesson—before going home.

Luckily we don't have any homework until the fourth grade.

I lease my basic equipment—skis, boots, and poles—from Sturtevant's. I'm still growing so it makes sense to do it this way.

When I get my boots fitted, I wear one pair of heavy ski socks with a nice smooth fit. I sit in a special chair with grips on each side so I can flex my knees forward as if I'm standing on skis.

What you want is just enough room to wiggle your toes, but the heel should be snug so your foot is held securely in the boot. This gives you better control over your skis.

I'm four feet five inches tall and my skis go up to my forehead. When I was just beginning to ski, my skis only went up to my chin. The poles have to be the right length too. When I hold the grips, my arms should be parallel to the ground.

They set the bindings according to your body weight and skiing ability. The bindings open and release your skis in case you fall so you won't get tangled up in them and injure yourself.

I take my skis in for a basic tune-up—we call that a "sharpen and wax"—whenever the edges get burred. That's when they're not as smooth as they should be. They can get roughed up when you hit rocks or other hard things in the snow. When this happens, your skis don't track as smoothly as they should.

I have a group lesson once a week after school. Juli Webb is our instructor. The first thing skiers do is buy a ski-lift ticket. I get a season pass so I don't have to do this every time I go skiing. School kids get a discount.

I put on Chap Stick with a sun filter in it because the wind and cold can dry your lips. I also put sunscreen on my face. Most skiers prefer goggles instead of dark glasses to protect their eyes from the sun because goggles fit better. It's very important to wear gloves, even if it's warm, because if you fall the ice crystals in the snow can cut your hands. When I'm ready, I step into my skis, check to be sure the bindings have snapped shut, and I'm off to the slopes.

Before we get on the ski lift, we review some basics.

Learning how to get up the mountain is just as important as learning how to ski down it. The way you go up is by sidestepping. Sidestepping on a mountain is a useful skill because you never know when you might have to go back up to retrieve a dropped pole or help a friend who has had a fall.

Juli has a special magic carpet so beginners can practice digging the uphill edges of their skis into the snow. I used it when I was starting to ski.

Bending your knees forward is how you get your balance, and balance is the name of the game.

We have one exercise holding our poles in front of us. It's called "driving the bus." This reminds me to keep my weight forward.

Knowing how to snowplow is very important because that's the surest way to slow down or stop. You do this by putting the tips of your skis together and "opening the back door." You make a V with your skis.

After we've worked on basics it's time to go up the mountain.

We stand in line for the lift. There's a marker to show you where to wait in line. There's another marker on the snow to show you where to wait for the chair.

You hold your poles in one hand so you'll be ready to grab the chair bar with the other one. It's very important to look for the chair bar so you can catch it as soon as it arrives. The chairs are moving all the time.

I love to look down at the skiers below. They look so tiny.

Sometimes Juli takes the lead when we ski down the mountain, and I try to copy her. We work on speed control.

We practice changing direction by going around poles we've planted in the snow.

Falling down is part of skiing and it's nothing to be scared of. Fighting a fall can make it worse because your body tenses up. Our teachers always tell us to just sit down and try and swing our skis below us. It sounds funny, but the better you ski, the more you fall. That's because the best skiers are always trying harder trails.

The Ski Patrol is always available if you need help. They bring injured skiers down on a snowmobile or toboggan.

On Thursday afternoons all the kids in ski school have races. We wear bibs with numbers on them so they can time us when we race.

The race course is defined by poles—or gates—and you have to ski around them on the way down. It's called "skiing through the course." There are three events in Alpine skiing: slalom, giant slalom, and downhill. My event is slalom, which consists of single-pole flags and lots of turns.

When I make a fast turn, I edge my skis a little more to slow down.

When I finish skiing, I put a ski tie on my skis to hold them together. It's easier to carry them that way. If I'm not going home right away, I put them on a ski rack so no one will trip over them.

At the end of the week everyone gets an achievement certificate after competing in the ski-school race.

We spend a lot of time with my grandparents who live nearby. My grandfather is the only member of the family who doesn't ski but he's a great cook. After a day on the slopes, I love pasta!

I try to be in bed by 8:00 P.M. I have a bulletin board over my bed where I hang all my ski-lift tickets and horse-show ribbons. I'm a member of our local pony club.

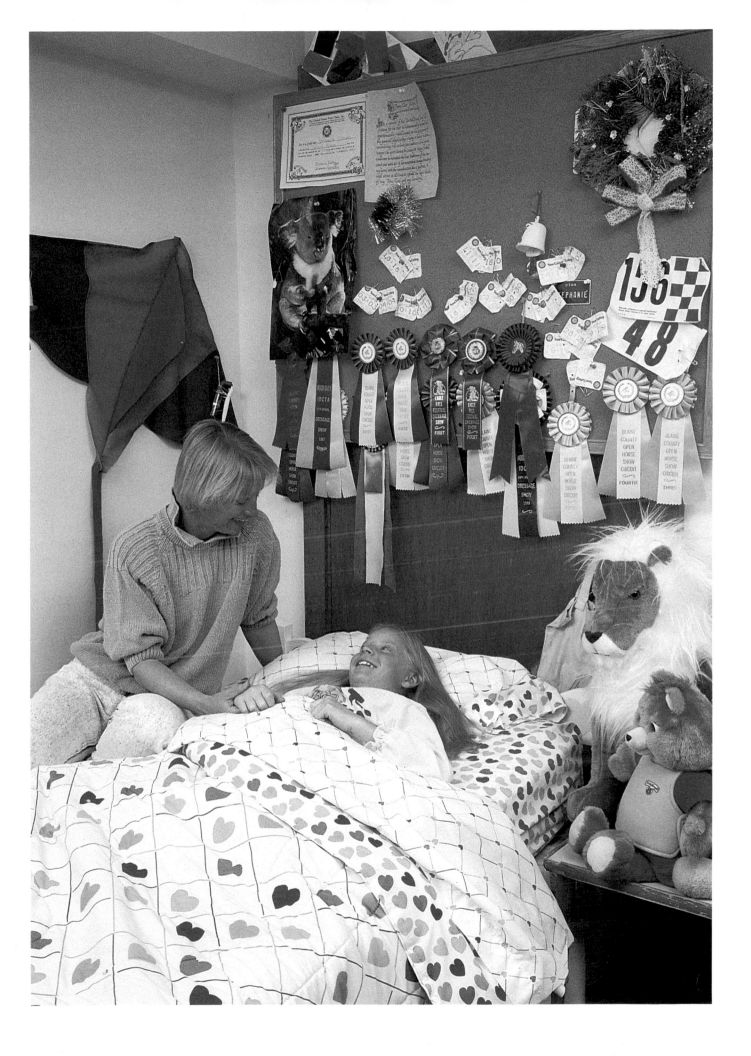

On Saturday mornings I ski with the D team. "D" stands for development. Our coaches are trying to develop our self-confidence and teach us the fundamentals of good technique, which we will build on over the coming years.

We race train on Baldy, which is the biggest ski mountain in Sun Valley. People come from all over the world to ski on it.

Between racing runs there's nothing like the excitement of "getting air" with jumps!

After the team skiing, I meet my dad at the top of Baldy and we ski together for the afternoon.

I always check the Information Center to see which runs have been groomed the night before. What grooming means is that when everyone is sleeping, there are people who go up and down the mountain on Snow-Cats, which look like big tractors. They rake and smooth the snow. Most people prefer a groomed run. Some skiers, including me, like the ungroomed slopes because we love skiing the bumps, which are called "moguls."

There's a trail map with a description of all the runs and a color code showing how difficult each one is.

Then Daddy and I talk about which way to go down.

We switch back and forth taking the lead down the mountain.

On Sundays and during vacations I do a lot of cross-country skiing.

You don't have to wear as many clothes when you cross-country because you work more. My mom is so good at sewing that she makes me Lycra tights to ski in.

You also wear lighter boots. They're soft and have flexible soles so you can lift your heels.

For cross-country skiing, they set tracks so it's easier to glide. They have a special place called Kinderland where they cut smaller tracks for kids. *Kinder* means children in German.

It's fun to follow our teacher, Hans. We all go in a single line to stay in the tracks.

Cross-country skiing was invented by people who lived where there was lots of snow. Of course they didn't have tracks so they had to break their own trails to get around.

Nordic Man and Nordic Woman are two magical cross-country characters who wear flowing capes and hats with wings. They just drop in. We never know when they're coming. The legend is that they ski through the air from Nordic Land to visit cross-country skiers. If the winds are strong or if there's too big a blizzard, they don't always make it.

Sometimes we have races with them or we play around Kinderland and the magical animals and castles. We ski under snakes and through forests of mushrooms. It helps us learn how to bend our knees, keep our balance, and make turns.

I love to ski cross-country with my grandmother. She's sixty-six but I have a hard time keeping up with her! We make our own trail—just like they did in the old days—through wintry woods and alongside beautiful streams.

One of the best things about ski resorts is that you can swim outdoors in heated pools—even in the winter. The water is from natural hot springs and is very warm. It feels terrific after you've been exercising all day.

Once a year we have a special race called the Kindercup. It's held on Dollar Mountain every March and only the local children can participate.

They post your class and racing order. This year I had to go first. This is hard because you can't watch your friends run the course before you.

Kids of all ages compete. They even have a class called P. A., which stands for Parental Assistance. Everyone races against the clock, and the fastest time wins.

Before it was my turn, I waited at the starting line. I tried to think about skiing my best.

Then the starter said, "Racer ready. Five, four, three, two, one … Go!"

Down I went as fast as I could.

The course was very icy.

They post the time after each racer crosses the finish line. My time was 46.74 seconds. I placed sixth!

After the races we all gathered at Dollar Cabin for the awards ceremony.

The top three winners in each class get trophies. They stand on a special platform, just like in the Olympics.

Everyone who races gets a Kindercup patch, even if they fall down or miss a gate. Mommy is going to sew mine on my parka.

Every year, after the Kindercup, our whole family goes on an old-fashioned sleigh ride through the woods. We bring a bale of hay and there's a place where we stop to feed the wild elk. We have a wonderful time.

Sun Valley is such a beautiful place and I'm very lucky to live here. Hope to see you on the slopes one day. Don't forget to bring your long underwear!